This book belongs to:

_____

_____

Make A Difference!

Grant Man___

Julie Cay M___

This book is dedicated to everyone
who listened to our story.

To the teachers, professors, counselors, grandparents,
moms, dads, brothers, sisters and many others whose
lives are touched by someone who is Different, but MORE!
Without your love and understanding, our journey in life
would be far more challenging. Thank you for seeing
MORE in us and guiding us along the way.

To my friends who are different like me,
remember you can always be more, not less.
Follow your passion, even if it seems *quirky*
to others.

We are Different...
so MAKE A DIFFERENCE!

~Grant Maniér

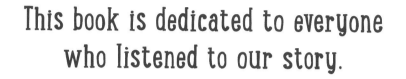

Foreword by Dr. Temple Grandin

Grant's artwork is a fabulous example of the creative work that a person with developmental differences can do. Educators need to put a greater emphasis on what students can do instead of what they cannot do. In my own case, my ability in art was always encouraged by my elementary school teachers. Art became the basis of my business designing livestock facilities.

Over the years, I have watched Grant develop both artistically and as a person. When he first started attending art shows, he was shy and had difficulty talking to people. Today, he loves to see people and discuss art. Getting out and doing art shows helped him to develop both his art and social skills. This book will show you how someone can be Different, but MORE!

DR. TEMPLE GRANDIN
Author, *Thinking in Pictures* and *The Autistic Brain*
HBO Biography: Temple Grandin
Time Magazine, 100 most influential people in the world
www.TempleGrandin.com

Grant teaching Temple to recycle and create Eco-Art

Tell your story through art: Jennifer Austin/Artist

Grant the Jigsaw Giraffe
Copyright © 2018 by Grant and Julie Maniér
All rights reserved
ISBN 978-1-941515-83-9
Library of Congress Control Number: 2017942708

Published by LongTale Publishing
www.LongTalePublishing.com
6824 Long Drive Houston, Texas 77087

Character illustrations and Eco-Art by Grant Maniér
Background illustrations by Depositphotos.com © interactimages
Design by Monica Thomas for TLC Graphics, www.TLCGraphics.com
In-house editor: Sharon Wilkerson

First Printing

The story and back cover text was set in 15 pt. Dyslexie Font, a dyslexia-friendly font. Dyslexie Font is designed to enhance reading abilities for people with dyslexia. Heavy baseline, varying ascending/descending links and semi-italics, among others, assures that the Dyslexie Font offers optimal reading comfort. Results may vary. For further information visit: www.DyslexieFont.com

GRANT
the Jigsaw Giraffe
Different is More®

Author: Julie Coy Maniér   Illustrator: Grant Maniér

LongTale
PUBLISHING

This is an exciting day at the city zoo. A new baby giraffe has just been born. His name is Grant.

Mama Jules checked Grant over and adored him from his head to his hooves, but something was different. His spots weren't spots! They were puzzles pieces, all jigsaw and brown. "He is something special, and I love him just the way he is," Mama Jules said.

One day, Ms. Judy, the macaw flew in to welcome the baby giraffe. Ms. Judy could talk and sing. "We all have talents like Ms. Judy. We just have to find them," said Mama Jules.

Ms. Judy admired Grant and said, "Puzzle pieces instead of spots? How unusual, but beautiful."

"Yes, he looks different than the other giraffes and sometimes acts different. But he has talent," said Mama Jules.

As Grant grew, his favorite thing to do was to admire the colorful trees, plants, flowers and animals. "Mama, how do I find my talent?" Grant asked one day.

"What inspires you, Grant?" she asked.

"I love colors," said Grant. "Look! Right here! How can I make these colors?" He studied the beautiful flowers.

Mama Jules smiled and said, "Grant, those are the colors of nature. Nature is art."

"Art?" asked Grant. "Yes, an artist uses a paintbrush to create the colors of the world," she explained.

"But I have hooves, so how will I hold a paintbrush?" he asked.

She said with a smile, "You will find a way. You're special. You're not less. You're more! Ms. Judy will take you around the zoo today to look for inspiration."

Along their walk, they came to the Orangutan village.

"What brings you out this way?" asked Tom.

"I need inspiration! I want to paint beautiful, colorful masterpieces. But, I can't hold a brush because I have hooves, and my body is a little awkward," Grant said sadly.

"Well Grant, I know something you can do that would be awesome," said Tom.

"Would you help me out with those yellow bananas high up in that tree? My swing isn't quite what it used to be."

"Yes sir, my neck can reach far and wide." Grant stretched his long neck and shook the bananas loose.

Tom shouted, "Yahoo, now that's talent! Grant, finding your talent takes time and effort, like a jigsaw puzzle. Yes, you're different...but, not less, you're MORE! Thanks for helping out an old guy like me."

While strolling down the lane, they met a beautiful peacock.

"Hello friends, what brings you out this way?" asked Peacock.

"Colors! I need inspiration!" said Grant with excitement.

"Well, I can show you some beautiful colors," said Peacock.

Peacock slowly spread his tail feathers. "They are my masterpiece," he said.

Grant admired the beauty and texture of all the colors.

Peacock said, "Grant, you know you have a masterpiece, too. Your puzzle markings are unique and beautiful. Yes, you're different...but, not less, you're MORE!"

Grant and Ms. Judy approached the Panda Village and saw a baby panda sleeping. "Oh, Hello!" said Panda.

"Did we wake you?" asked Ms. Judy.

"No, I was meditating. I need to find my creativity to solve my problem."

"Creativity, like an artist?" asked Grant.

"Yes, exactly," said Panda.

"So what seems to be the problem?" asked Grant.

"Well, see those delicious red apples hanging in that tree? They look so good to eat, but mother says I am not to climb the fence," Panda sighed.

"I will help you out," said Grant. He walked over to the fence and using his long sticky tongue, he plucked some apples for his friend to enjoy.

"Eureka! Problem solved. Grant, you have talent and you are creative. Yes, you're different...but, not less, you're MORE!" said Panda.

Grant and Ms. Judy made their last stop at the Owl Sanctuary.

"It seems you're looking for something," said the wise owl.

"How did you know?" asked Grant.

"I heard about you from the other zoo animals," said Owl.

"You heard I want to be a talented artist, but that I can't hold a paintbrush...because I have hooves?" asked Grant.

"Grant, there are many ways to paint a masterpiece. Your hooves and everything about you might be just what you need," said Owl. "You'll find your inspiration, and it will be special, just like you. Grant, you're different...but, not less, you're MORE!"

Each day, **Grant** searched for ways to become an artist while using his creativity, his physical abilities and his unique beauty as inspiration.

One day while walking along the zoo fence, **Grant** saw something he had never seen before.

"What is that?" asked Grant.

Ms. Judy flew in for a closer look. "Recycled magazines. That's trash...it's not at all pretty."

"Look at all the colors! I know just how to reuse this recycled paper!" he shouted out.

Grant needed the perfect canvas. Being creative, he chose the white fence. Then he thought, *How will I tear all of this paper? Oh, yes! My HOOVES!* Piece by piece, he tore the paper and placed the colors into piles.

Next, he used his sticky tongue to lick the paper and his long neck to stroke the paper onto the fence. He worked on his art for hours. Ms. Judy couldn't believe what she saw.

Soon, Mr. Becker, the zookeeper came by and peeked over the fence. He asked, "What are you working on, Grant?"

"Recycled art!" Grant shouted.

"What a great idea, and you're helping the environment. It looks like you are just about out of paper. I'll spread the word and gather up more recycled materials for you."

The zoo announced a recycle drive for Grant's eco-friendly project. Schools, neighborhoods and businesses had puzzle drives and filled recycle bins with calendars, wallpaper and much more.

"What are you going to call this art, Grant?" asked Ms. Judy.

"Well, I am using cool colors, cool shapes and cool textures. I will call my art, *COOLAGES*," said Grant with a smile.

Mr. Becker was curious to see how Grant used the recycled materials. He walked behind the fence and could not believe his eyes.

"WOW! Grant it's a masterpiece! You're a talented artist, indeed! Let's have an Art Exhibit. It will be for all to see!" he shouted.

Mama Jules was there to support and encourage Grant. She always knew her son was going to do something amazing!

People from all over the city came to see Grant's masterpieces. They were proud to be a part of his recycling project and share his artwork around the world.

Grant found his talent and inspiration thanks to his zoo friends and an eco-friendly environment.

Grant named each piece after his friends. Tom, The Gentle Giant, Peacock Lane, Baby M.M.O.B, Caribbean Owl and Ms. Judy.

Grant used over 60,000 pieces of recycled materials at his exhibit: magazines, wallpaper, calendars, posters, beads, hairpins, jewelry, pressed wood, stationary paper, business cards and puzzles.

Grant the Jigsaw Giraffe made such an impression throughout the world with his eco-art project. He received the *Best Recycling Program Award* for his dedication to teach others to be environmentally responsible and to keep our Earth green and clean.

Grant knew he was different, but that did not stop him. He chased his dream and became a talented artist.

Every day reminding himself...*It's not what I can't do, it's what I can do that makes me MORE!*

Different is MORE®

Grant Maniér
Artist ~ Special Needs Advocate ~ Public Speaker

Today's world is evolving into an eco-friendly environment and Grant Maniér (maun-yay), a young talented eco-artist living with autism, has incorporated conservationism into his work. Reduce, Reuse, and Recycle is the foundation for Grant's art. Grant creates works of art using magazines, calendars, wallpaper, posters, puzzles and more. Each art contains thousands of cut/torn pieces of recycled materials. Using cool colors, cool shapes, cool textures, Grant calls his masterpieces, *COOLAGES*.

Grant has received honors for his advocacy work, been featured at events, has been seen on TV and featured in newspapers, magazines and social media articles. Grant focuses on educating children and adults about the importance of environmental responsibility through his successful outreach program.

Grant Maniér
Grant the Jigsaw Giraffe Creator

For more information visit: **www.JigsawGrant.com** and **www.GrantsEcoArt.com**

Grant, The Jigsaw Giraffe Plush Toy

About the Author & Illustrator

Grant and Julie Coy Maniér (maun-yay) have spent six years building Grant's Eco-Art business. They travel and teach environmental responsibility and raise the awareness of special talents.

Grant, who lives with autism, has had an obsession for paper since childhood. Instead of suppressing his obsessive behavior, Julie re-directed his amazing ability to focus and orchestrate colors into something constructive, recycling and collaging to create unique art masterpieces. Since Grant was fifteen years old, his art has been captivating audiences from all over the world. He is an award-winning artist who displays his art exhibit at events, conferences, schools and fundraisers. Grant's mission is to keep our Earth green and clean and to teach audiences that ... *Different, is MORE!*

Chelsea Williams Photography

Coming Soon

Over the years, Julie has watched Grant grow into an amazing young man and artist, who inspires and shifts perceptions of how people stereotype special needs individuals. Grant's journey inspired Julie to write a children's book about Grant, but as a giraffe! With Eco-Art involved, you will be amazed as you read how the story of a giraffe and Grant Maniér are one in the same.

This book is not about having autism ... it's about seeing the different abilities in everyone.

Books by Julie and Grant Maniér:
Eco-Impressionism: The Paper Palette Artist
Dear Journal, I Have Autism

Thank you for making this book MORE!

Dr. Temple Grandin	Kulture City	Jennifer Allen	Laurence & Rosanne Becker
Susie Palacios	Larry Bain	Steve and Geselle Polakoff	Kerry & Henry Tucker
Regina Rash, CPA	Dr. Marcia Laviage	Ghostwriters on Call	Donny and Darla Farmer
Pam Tipton	Andrea Schmauss	Vaughn Lauer	Impulse Art, Paul Boutte
Ann & John Zdansky	Edith Gibson	Kelly Wallace Moselage	Cherry Tree Republicans
Jane and John Fayland	Wendy Dawson	Christopher Cardenas	QB Pro Office Services
Reen and Lydia Williams	Focus Academy	Jennifer Austin/Artist	Moffett & Company Properties
Tim Paul, State Farm	Tori Rash	Social Motion Skills	Turtle Wing Foundation
World Photo, LLC	A New You	Diann Boehm	Chelsea Williams Photography
The ART of Autism	Dan Gillingham	Rose and Martin Coy	Bellaire Family Eye Care
Tom and Sonia Deuble	Robin Rettie, LLR	Kate Bauer, Attorney	Dyslexia Font, Christian Boer
Chip Vanghundy Show	Campbell Concrete	WISE Conference	LongTale Publishing
Night of Superstars	I Promote You	Aspergers101.org	UncoverHTX.com (Digital app.)
Jeanna TenBrink	Ignite the Secret	Westview School	STAPLES (Spring, TX #1498)

PartnERs Emergency Center   **Howard Nations Law Firm**